# Claude Debussy

Universal
Saxophone
Edition

## Saxophone Album
arranged for Alto Saxophone and Piano
by James Rae

General Editor
John Harle

## Saxophon-Album
für Altsaxophon und Klavier
bearbeitet von James Rae

Universal Edition UE 17 777
ISMN 979-0-008-01088-0
UPC 8-03452-00270-3
ISBN 978-3-7024-0514-4

## Preface

This album has been compiled and arranged with the prime intention of providing saxophonists with the opportunity of playing a wide variety of music by Debussy.

The pieces chosen are of moderate difficulty satisfying the needs of both student and professional alike. They also help to bridge the "repertoire gap" between the very elementary and the very advanced, as most of the material available for saxophone today seems to fall into these categories.

These pieces are musically very satisfying as the style of Debussy lends itself so well to the saxophone. It is unfortunate that Debussy discovered the instrument so late in life as otherwise I am sure that he would have graced us with more original material.

James Rae

## Vorwort

Die vorliegende Sammlung von Bearbeitungen für Saxophon wurde in erster Linie zu dem Zweck zusammengestellt, den Spielern dieses Instruments die Möglichkeit zu bieten, eine breite Auswahl der Musik Debussys vorzutragen.

Die Stücke sind als mittelschwer einzustufen und werden den Erwartungen sowohl des Schülers als auch des Berufsmusikers gerecht. Weiters sollen sie dazu beitragen, die „Repertoirelücke" zwischen sehr einfachem und sehr schwerem Material zu überbrücken, zumal die meisten Stücke, die dem Saxophonisten heute zur Verfügung stehen, in eine dieser beiden Katogorien fallen.

Musikalisch gesehen sind die vorliegenden Stücke äußerst ergiebig, da sich der Stil Debussys für das Saxophon hervorragend eignet. Es ist sehr zu bedauern, daß Debussy dieses Instrument erst in seinen letzten Lebensjahren entdeckte; er hätte uns sonst zweifellos eine größere Anzahl an eigens für das Saxophon komponierten Werken hinterlassen.

J. R.

# 1. Le petit nègre

Claude Debussy
(1862-1918)
arr. James Rae

**Allegro giusto**

Universal Edition No. 17777

4

## 2. Arabesque No.1

Andantino con moto

99

103

## 3. Élégie

**Lent et douloureux**

*p cantabile espr.*

*un poco mosso*

12

## 4. Petite pièce

**Modéré et doucement rythmé**

## 5. Danse Bohémienne

## 6. La plus que lente

**Lent** (*molto rubato con morbidezza*)

# 7. The little Shepherd

**Très modéré**

*plus mouvementé*

*au mouv^t*     *cédez*

*au mouv^t*

## 8. Jimbo's Lullaby

**Assez modéré**

## 9. La fille aux cheveux de lin

## 10. Golliwogg's cake walk

**Allegro giusto**